Stop That Nose!

by **Martha Peaslee Levine**

illustrated by **Lee White**

Marshall Cavendish Children

Marshall Cavendish Corporation, 99 White Plains Road, Tarrytown, NY 10591
www.marshallcavendish.us

Library of Congress Cataloging-in-Publication Data
Levine, Martha Peaslee.
Stop that nose! / by Martha Peaslee Levine ; illustrated by Lee White. — 1st ed.
p. cm.
Summary: When young David's father loses his nose after a particularly hearty sneeze, it takes a chase and an airplane ride before the naughty nose can be returned to its rightful face.
ISBN-13:978-0-7614-5280-5
ISBN-10:0-7614-5280-x
[1. Nose—Fiction. 2. Sneezing—Fiction. 3. Humorous stories. 4. Stories in rhyme.] I. White, Lee, 1970- ill. II. Title.
PZ8.3.L5775Sto 2006
[E]—dc22
2005004088

The text of this book is set in Neutra.
The illustrations are rendered in oil on watercolor paper.
Book design by Becky Terhune

Printed in China
First edition
1 3 5 6 4 2

To David and Dayna, whose love and talents always blow me away

And to Rich, who helped inspire this book, even though his sneezes haven't blown off his nose—yet
—M. P. L.

To my wife, Lisa; my mom, Gerre; and my grandmother, Anne
—L. W.

"A-A-ACHOO!"

Dad sneezed a huge sneeze
that blew off his nose in a hurricane breeze.

"Dad!" yelled David. "There goes your nose!"
"Catch it!" cried Dad. "Before it blows!"
David's flying tackle missed its mark.
That naughty nose sneezed, **"A-A-Aardvark!"**

"Stop!" called David, but the nose
started running.

Trying to catch the runaway nose,
David got tangled in a line of clothes.

He grabbed for the nose and shouted, "Freeze!"
But the nose had already started to sneeze.
Inside a shirt, the nose snorted some soap.
Loud as a bugle, it sneezed, **"A-A-Antelope!"**

"Stop!" called David, but the nose kept running.

It bounced and jounced into thick prickly plants,
then wheezed and sneezed, **"A-A-Ambulance!"**

"Stop!" called David, but the nose kept running.

The ambulance, thumping down the road,
bumped a chicken truck, dumping its load.
The trucks slowed down to a skidding halt
and sent the nose off in a somersault.

AMBULANCE

David yanked open the ambulance door.
The nose was skipping across the floor.
Nuzzling the muddy accelerator,
the nose snorted and sneezed, **"A-A-Alligator!"**

Alligator and nose scampered away.
Dad's nose just wouldn't obey!
It stopped at a fruit stand, snuffled a grape.
Crinkling up, it sneezed, **"A-A-Ape!"**

"Stop!" called David, but the nose kept running.

The ape climbed a building way up in the air
with the nose clutched tight to its shaggy hair.
Above the roof, nose and ape held tight
to an antenna with a blinking light.

David shouted, as he started to climb,
"Please, nose, come down. It's dinnertime!"
He snagged the ape's big furry toe,
but the nose decided it was time to go.

Maybe it smelled the first drops of rain.
Wrinkling up, it sneezed, **"A-A-Airplane!"**

"Stop!" called David, but the nose kept running.

David leapt for the airplane and above its roar
shouted, "Please, nose, don't sneeze anything more."
But sniffing the back of the pilot's seat,
the nose suddenly sneezed, **"A-A-Athlete!"**

This time the nose was a super sprayer.
Out popped a gigantic basketball player.

23

The basketball player was very fast.
He snagged that runaway nose at last.
He dribbled the dribbling, wiggling nose,
while into the clouds the airplane rose.
The athlete yelled, "Who wants this nose back?"
"I do," cried Dad from the cul-de-sac.

The plane landed in David's backyard.
"You caught my nose!" Dad cheered. "Was it hard?"
David said, "Dad, your nose kept running;
but as you can see, I was more cunning."

David slapped the nose back into place,
right in the middle of Dad's noseless face.
Dad pulled David into a big bear hug,
the kind where you're held all nice and snug.

Then all of a sudden Dad started to sniff.
David reached in his pants for a handkerchief.

He braced himself, ready to run,
in case this sneeze was another big one.
No matter how much this nose might spray,
David would not let it get away.

"A-A-A. . . ." Here the sneeze came.
Would it be violent or tame?
"A-A. . . ." The sneeze grew and grew.

Just a normal-sized Dad sneeze. Phew!
So David just said, "God bless you."